The Mystery Guest

Written by

Tony Bradman

Illustrated by

John Wallace

PUFFIN BOOKS

For Rufus – meow!
T. B.

For Jude
J. W.

PUFFIN BOOKS

Published by the Penguin Group
Penguin Books Ltd, 80 Strand, London WC2R 0RL, England
Penguin Putnam Inc., 375 Hudson Street, New York, New York 10014, USA
Penguin Books Australia Ltd, 250 Camberwell Road, Camberwell, Victoria 3124, Australia
Penguin Books Canada Ltd, 10 Alcorn Avenue, Toronto, Ontario, Canada M4V 3B2
Penguin Books India (P) Ltd, 11 Community Centre, Panchsheel Park, New Delhi – 110 017, India
Penguin Books (NZ) Ltd, Cnr Rosedale and Airborne Roads, Albany, Auckland, New Zealand
Penguin Books (South Africa) (Pty) Ltd, 24 Sturdee Avenue, Rosebank 2196, South Africa

Penguin Books Ltd, Registered Offices: 80 Strand, London WC2R 0RL, England

www.penguin.com

First published 2001
3 5 7 9 10 8 6 4 2

Text copyright © Tony Bradman, 2001
Illustrations copyright © John Wallace, 2001
All rights reserved

The moral right of the author and illustrator has been asserted

Set in Frutiger

Manufactured in China

British Library Cataloguing in Publication Data
A CIP catalogue record for this book is available from the British Library

ISBN 0–140–56749–6

I went to a fancy dress party ...

… And all my friends were there
Two dressed up as vampires,
One dressed as a bear.

Jason was a penguin
With a very silly nose,
And Molly was a fairy
Who liked to tread on toes.

Neil was being Wonder Man,
Tracey was a stone,
Sarah was a rubbish bin –
We all left her alone!

Tony was a Frankenstein,
His teeth and eyes were red.
"What an ugly mask!" we shouted ...
"But it's my face," he said.

Everyone was having fun,
We played games on the floor …
Neil was winning, then we heard
A knocking on the door.

Someone coming to the party,
Someone coming late.
He certainly had a costume on,
Although it looked a state.

He seemed to be an alien,
With lots of bulging eyes.
But those tentacles looked terrible.
He'd never win a prize.

He sat right next to Sarah,
Despite the awful smell,
Then ate a plate of sausages,
And fourteen cakes as well.

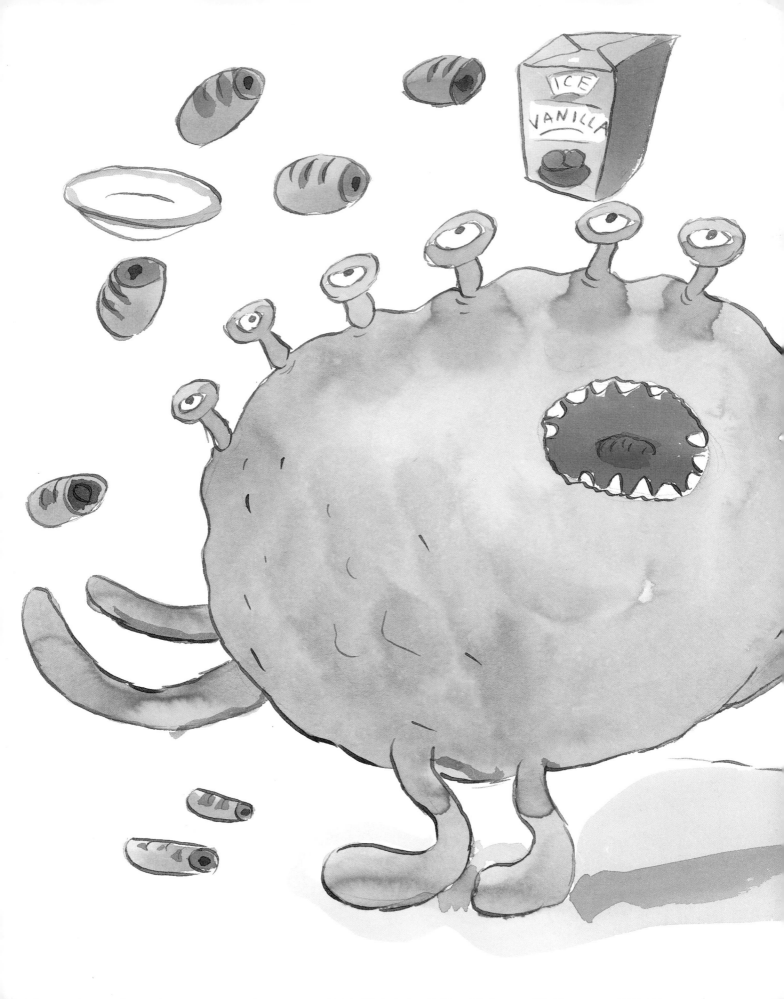

He ate a plate of sausage rolls,
And then he couldn't wait ...
He ate the ice cream in the fridge,
And then he ate ... a plate!

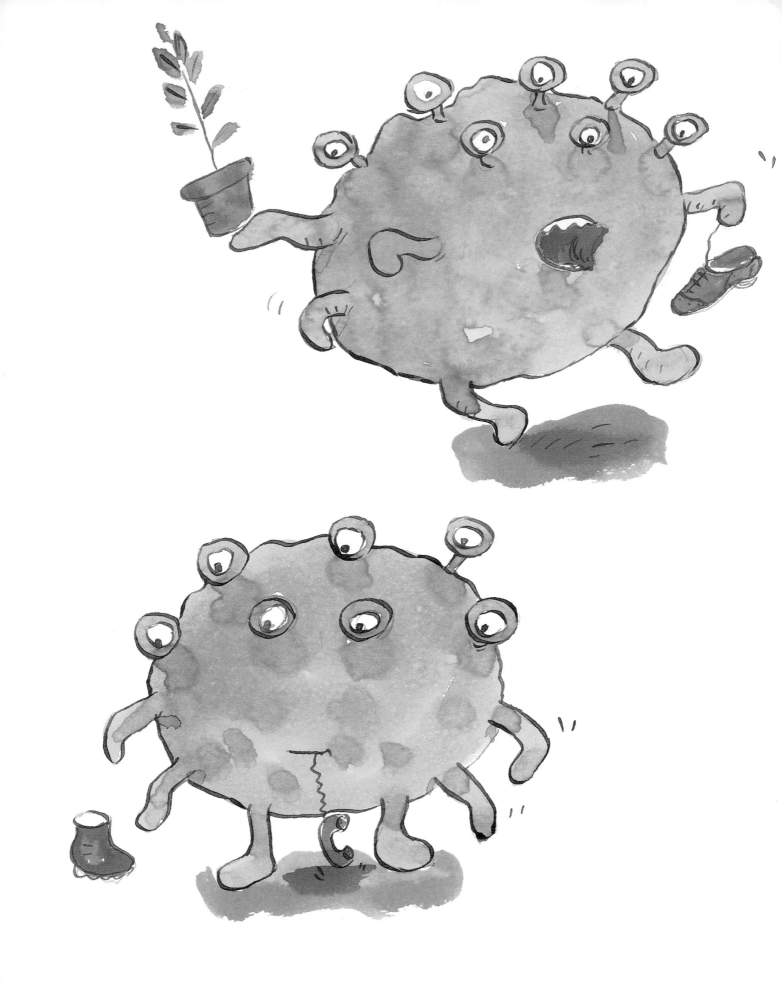

He ate a lot of other things –
A plant, a shoe, a phone.
He was good at pass the parcel …
He played it all alone!

But he joined in with the other games,
He just loved hide-and-seek!
And when we found him all he did
Was bleep and buzz and squeak.

Nothing much else happened ...
Except to Lee's surprise
We voted for the best-dressed guest –
And Tracey won the prize!

And now the fun was over,
Our mums and dads arrived,
All complaining of the thing
Blocking up the drive.

It was some kind of vehicle,
With red lights all around.
It had no wheels but hovered,
Just above the ground.

But Neil had lost his party hat,
And Tracey fought with Lee.
Sarah didn't want to go,
And turned on the TV.

No one really listened
When a man on TV said
That something had been spotted,
Something fast, and red ...

By the time we got outside,
The vehicle thing had gone.
Where it had been there was a hole
As deep as it was long.

No one took much notice;
We all went on our way ...
But who was that dressed as an alien?

Who invited him anyway?